13th March '06

D0115296

THE POW PUFF PUZZLE

Dear Niku,

We love you.

Tikku, Parth,
Nayanakaki & Rajeshkaka

YEARLING BOOKS/YOUNG YEARLINGS/YEARLING CLASSICS are designed especially to entertain and enlighten young people. Patricia Reilly Giff, consultant to this series, received her bachelor's degree from Marymount College and a master's degree in history from St. John's University. She holds a Professional Diploma in Reading and a Doctorate of Humane Letters from Hofstra University. She was a teacher and reading consultant for many years, and is the author of numerous books for young readers.

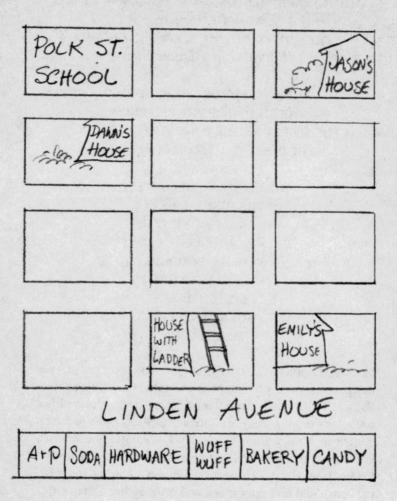

THE POWDER PUFF PUZZLE

Patricia Reilly Giff

Illustrated by Blanche Sims

A YOUNG YEARLING BOOK

Published by
Bantam Doubleday Dell Books for Young Readers
a division of
Bantam Doubleday Dell Publishing Co. Inc.
1540 Broadway
New York, New York 10036

If you purchased this book without a cover you should be aware that this book is stolen property. It was reported as "unsold and destroyed" to the publisher and neither the author nor the publisher has received any payment for this "stripped book."

Text copyright © 1987 by Patricia Reilly Giff
Illustrations copyright © 1987 by Blanche Sims

All rights reserved. No part of this book may be reproduced or transmitted in any form or by any means, electronic or mechanical, including photo-copying, recording, or by any information storage and retrieval system, without the written permission of the Publisher, except where permitted by law.

The trademarks Yearling® and Dell® are registered in the U.S. Patent and Trademark Office and in other countries.

ISBN: 0-440-47180-X

Printed in the United States of America

December 1987

23 22 21 20 19 18 17 16 15 14

Love and welcome to
James Patrick Giff,
August 5, 1987

··· CHAPTER 1 ···

Dawn Bosco was hot.

There was no shade in the yard. Not one bit.

Then she remembered.

Emily Arrow had a pool. A nice cool one.

She looked around. "Come on, Powder Puff," she yelled. "We're going to Emily's house."

She looked up at the fence.

"Powder Puff?"

Where was he? She dived under the bushes. "Where are you?"

The cat jumped at her.

"Whew," Dawn said. "I thought you were lost."

She scooped him up.

Powder Puff was the greatest cat in the world.

He was all black. Almost all black.

He had one white ear.

He had a white tip on his tail.

Noni, Dawn's grandmother, looked up. She was weeding the yard.

"We have more weeds than tomatoes," she said. She rubbed her back.

Dawn put Powder Puff over her shoulders.

He curled his tail around her neck. "This cat's perfect," she said.

She gave the white tip of his tail a tug.

The cat began to purr. He sounded like the refrigerator.

"This cat's a pest," said Noni. "Last night

he jumped on my bed. I woke up. I saw those yellow eyes."

Noni shivered. "Whoosh. I thought he was a tiger."

"You should have called me," Dawn said. "I'm not afraid of anything."

"Really?" said Noni.

"It's because I'm a detective," Dawn said.

Noni stood up. "Ouch, my knees. The ground is hard."

"I'll rub them," Dawn said. She smiled. Noni's knees were ticklish.

"No, thanks," said Noni.

"We're going to Emily Arrow's," Dawn said. "Me and Powder Puff."

Noni shook her head. "Better not take the cat. He'll get lost."

Dawn stuck out her lip. "He wants to come."

Noni slapped at a fly.

Smack.

The cat jumped at the noise.

He jumped off Dawn's shoulder.

"Hey," Dawn said.

The cat raced out of the yard.

Dawn ran after him.

"See what I mean?" Noni called.

"Powder Puff," Dawn yelled.

The cat kept going. He went up one block. He went down the next.

Dawn kept going too.

The cat dashed across the street.

A horn sounded. The cat went faster. He raced for the next street.

"Yeow," Dawn yelled. "Watch out."

The light turned red. The cars stopped.

Dawn started across the street.

The cat was halfway down the block.

His back was up. His tail was out.

A red car was parked in front of the hardware store. A mess of a red car.

One fender had dents.

The paint was scratched.

Powder Puff jumped up on the hood.

He put his paws on the side mirror.

He jumped in the open window.

"Powder Puff," Dawn yelled again.

Just then a woman came down the street.

She was carrying a box. It looked heavy.

She had a pole over her shoulder.

She was long and skinny like the pole.

A jelly cookie was between her teeth.

She had a gray ponytail. A long skinny one.

It looked like a mousetail.

She opened the car door. She shoved the
pole in.

"Lady," Dawn yelled.

The light turned green. The woman
slammed the car door.

All the cars started to move.

The red one pulled out.

Dawn started to run.

Powder Puff must be on the backseat. The woman didn't even know he was there.

"Stop," Dawn shouted.

A horn blared in back of her.

Dawn jumped out of the way.

She raced to the curb. She kept watching the red car.

It was moving slowly.

She looked at the license plate. Detectives were supposed to do that.

It began with a *P*.

Dawn shaded her eyes. *P* . . . and then *A* . . . All letters.

A name.

She had to see it.

The car started to turn the corner.

Dawn took three steps.

It was too late.

The car was gone.

So was Powder Puff.

··· CHAPTER 2 ···

Dawn went down the street.

She didn't look where she was going.

She fell over a ladder.

"Ouch," she said. She could feel tears in her eyes.

She turned the corner.

Jason Basyk was standing in front of Emily's house.

So was Alex Walker.

They were wearing bathing suits. Wet ones.

Jason was jumping up and down. He turned his head to one side. "Water in my ears," he said.

"My cat," Dawn said. "My poor cat."

She sat down on the grass. She tried to stop crying.

"What happened?" Alex asked.

"He rode away in a car," said Dawn. "He's lost."

Jason stopped jumping. "You'll find him."

"No." Dawn shook her head. "He's far away."

Alex shook his head too. "You're right. He's gone."

"Don't be silly," Jason said.

Dawn looked up.

"You forgot," Jason told Alex. "Dawn's a detective." He started to jump again.

Alex put a towel around his neck. "Hey, that's right."

"Of course," said Dawn. "I'm not worried. Not one bit."

She swallowed.

"What are you going to do?" Jason asked.

Dawn tried to think. Poor Powder Puff. He liked to eat potato chips. He liked applesauce too.

The woman in the car didn't know that.

Suppose she didn't even see him?

Suppose she locked the door with the cat inside?

Dawn wouldn't think about that. She'd think about how to find him.

"I tried to see the license plate," Dawn said.

"What was it?" Jason asked.

"A name. It began with *P*. There was an *A* in it too."

"How many letters?" Jason asked.

"What kind of name?" Alex said at the same time.

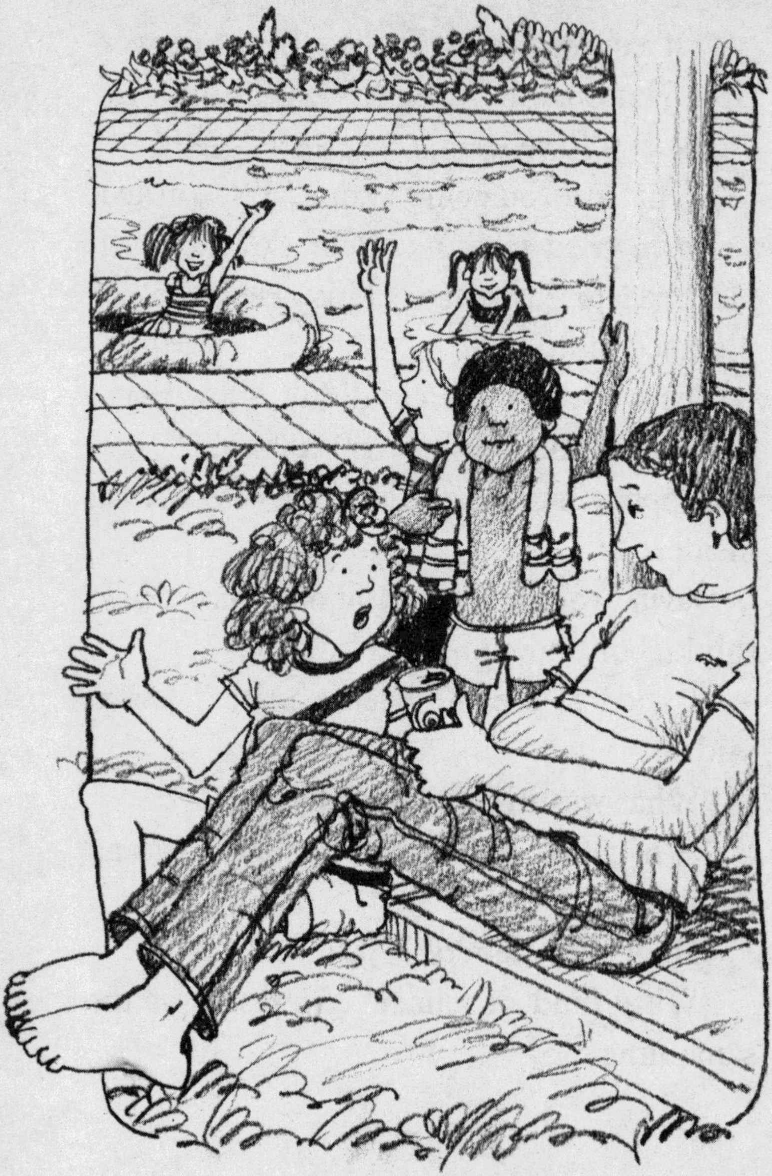

Dawn shook her head. "I don't know."

She pulled at a piece of grass. "A woman got into the car. Maybe it was a woman's name."

"Good thinking," said Alex.

"A woman's name beginning with P . . ." Dawn began to chew on the piece of grass.

"Peg," said Jason. "Like my sister Peggy."

"I don't think Peggy drives," Alex said.

The boys grinned at each other.

"Uh-uh. Not Peg," Dawn said. It has an A. Remember?"

"Patsy," said Alex. "That's my aunt's name."

"Pamela," said Jason. "That's my aunt's name."

Dawn sat up straight. "Maybe."

"What's next?" Alex asked.

"I have to see Emily Arrow's father. He's a policeman."

Alex rubbed his face with his towel. "You're lucky. Mr. Arrow is off today. He's in the backyard."

They went around the side of the house.

Emily was in the pool.

So was Stacy, her little sister.

Stacy was singing a song.

Emily was floating on her yellow raft.

It was too big for the pool.

It kept bumping the side.

Mr. Arrow was sitting on the back step. He was drinking a can of soda.

Emily sat down next to him.

"My favorite detective," he said.

Stacy stuck her head over the side of the pool. "No, I am."

"You too," said Mr. Arrow.

Dawn told him about Powder Puff. She told him about the license plate.

"It said Pamela," said Alex.

"Or Patsy," said Jason.

"What color was the plate?" Mr. Arrow asked.

Dawn frowned. "It was white. White with blue letters." She nodded. "It had a picture of the Statue of Liberty."

"That's New York," said Mr. Arrow.

He took a last drink of soda. "I'll find out." He went into the house.

Jason looked at Dawn. "How—"

"Policemen know the license plates. There's a list."

"That must be a long list," said Alex.

"Very," said Dawn. "Mr. Arrow will call the police station. A policeman will look it up."

Alex crossed his fingers.

So did Jason.

Dawn crossed her toes.

A little later Mr. Arrow came outside. He was frowning.

"No Pamela," he said.

"How about—" Jason began.

Mr. Arrow shook his head. "No Patsy."

Dawn wanted to cry. She stood up. "I have to go home now."

Emily waved at her. "Don't you want a quick dip? Just to cool off?"

Dawn started down the path. She tried to smile. "Not now."

She waved back at them. "Thanks," she told Mr. Arrow.

She heard Emily say, "Poor Dawn."

She heard Stacy say, "Poor Powder Puff."

She started to run.

Powder Puff was gone forever.

··· CHAPTER 3 ···

"Dawn Bosco," a voice called. "Wait a minute."

Dawn stopped.

She turned around.

Stacy Arrow was running down the street.

Her feet were bare.

She was running on her tiptoes.

"My father says come back," Stacy yelled.

Dawn blinked hard. "All right."

They started back.

They had to go slowly.

"Ouch, my poor feet," Stacy kept saying.

Mr. Arrow was waiting for them. He had a pile of big papers.

He had a bunch of crayons.

He smiled when he saw Dawn. "I have an idea."

"To find my cat?" Dawn asked.

"It might help," said Mr. Arrow. "I'm not sure."

He called Emily out of the pool. "Dry off," he said. "We need everyone."

Stacy shook herself. "I'm drying off too." They sat down at the table: Dawn and Stacy, Jason and Alex, Emily and Mr. Arrow.

"We'll make signs," said Mr. Arrow. "We'll let everyone know. Someone may have seen Powder Puff."

"Good," said Stacy. "I'll write my name."

Mr. Arrow shook his head. "We're going to write Powder Puff's name."

Stacy frowned. "I don't know how to write Powder Puff. You forgot. I didn't start school yet."

Emily looked as if she were going to laugh. She didn't though. "Just make a cat. I'll write the words."

Everyone drew a picture of Powder Puff.

Dawn drew a fat Powder Puff.

He had one white ear.

He had a white tip on his tail.

Emily drew a skinny Powder Puff.

Jason drew a long one.

Mr. Arrow watched. "Terrific," he told Dawn.

"Mine's terrific too," said Stacy.

Mr. Arrow nodded. "Now," he said. "Write LOST on top."

Jason wrote a red LOST.

Alex wrote a yellow LOST.

Stacy wrote a blue LSTO.

They wrote Dawn's name underneath.

They wrote her address too.

Mr. Arrow helped Stacy with hers.

Then he stood up. "Now put these signs all over the place."

Dawn piled the signs up. "Thanks," she said. "I'll bet we'll find him now."

"Hey," said Jason. "What time is it?"

Mr. Arrow looked at his watch. "Lunchtime."

Dawn put the signs under her arm. "I've got to hurry. Noni will be looking for me."

She started down the driveway.

"Wait," yelled Emily Arrow.

She rushed after Dawn.

She had a pack of thumbtacks.

"Thanks," Dawn said again.

She started down the street.

"Come for a swim," Emily called. "Come when you find Powder Puff."

Dawn waved back with one hand. "Don't worry. I will. I'm dying of the heat."

She stopped at the corner.

She tacked Jason's sign to a pole.

On the next street she put another sign.

She kept going. She passed the house with the ladder. She stepped around it.

By the time she reached home, the signs were gone.

She stood there.

Suppose the lady with the mousetail didn't live near here?

Suppose she didn't see the signs?

Dawn would have to do something else to find Powder Puff.

But what?

··· CHAPTER 4 ···

Dawn sat at the kitchen table. "I'm not hungry."

Noni pinched her cheek. "Maybe the cat will find his way back."

"Maybe he won't," Dawn said.

"Eat some egg salad," said Noni. "Have a potato chip."

"I can't," Dawn said.

Noni sighed. "You want to look like a skinny little toothpick?"

Dawn gave Noni a kiss.

She went outside.

Powder Puff wasn't in the yard.

He wasn't in the street.

Dawn sighed.

How could she find him?

Jason came along. He was dragging a stick on the ground.

"What's that for?" Dawn asked.

Jason raised one shoulder. "It's a sword."

"Don't poke anyone in the eye."

"Uh-uh." Jason dropped the stick. "I have nothing to do."

"Help me find Powder Puff."

Jason sat on the curb. "How?"

Dawn looked up in the air. "We could look for the car. The red car."

"It's hot," Jason said. "Too hot to walk all over the place."

Dawn looked worried. "Maybe Powder Puff is thirsty."

"You're right," said Jason. "I'll help."

He grabbed his stick.

They started down the street.

Dawn looked back at the house. "I'm going for a walk," she shouted.

Jason looked back. "I don't think Noni heard you."

Dawn raised one shoulder. "Just as long as I said where I'm going."

Jason didn't say anything. He rolled his eyes.

Dawn sighed. "Wait a minute."

She raced back to the house. "Noni," she yelled.

Noni stuck her head out the window.

"I'm going for a walk," Dawn said. "Jason and me."

"Don't go far."

Dawn shook her head. She ran back to Jason.

They started down the street again.

They turned the corner.

Four cars were parked on the next block.

Two black ones.

A green station wagon.

One red car.

"Is that it?" Jason asked.

Dawn shook her head. "The other one was a mess. A big mess."

"Just like that house," Jason said.

Dawn looked up.

It was the house with the ladder.

The ladder wasn't on the sidewalk anymore. It was against the house. A gray, dirty house.

"I guess they're going to paint," Dawn said.

"Let's try the next block," Jason said. He pointed with his stick. "Forward march."

"Hey, wait a minute." He reached into his pocket. He pulled out two candy kisses.

"Too hot in my pocket," he said. "They're all soft. Want one?"

"Maybe." Dawn held out one hand.

She pulled off the silver paper.

She popped the candy into her mouth.

"Gooey," she said. She rubbed her hands together.

They were full of chocolate.

On the next street were nine cars.

Not one red one.

There were no red cars on the street after that either.

"I'm dying for a glass of water," Dawn said.

"I'm dying for an ice cube," Jason said. He waved his stick over his head. "Two ice cubes."

He looked down the next block. "One ice cube for my mouth. The other one for the top of my head."

They started down Stone Street.

"Hey," Dawn said.

She stopped.

She pointed up at a white house. "Look."

Jason stopped too.

"There in the window," she said.

"A cat," said Jason. "A black one."

"Powder Puff," Dawn yelled.

The cat looked at them. He stood up on the windowsill.

He waved his long black tail.

"Come on," Dawn yelled. "Let's get him."

Jason shook his head. "Wait a minute."

"No. Don't wait," Dawn said. "Hurry."

She raced up the front path.

···CHAPTER 5···

Dawn rang the bell.

Once. Twice.

Nobody answered.

The cat sat in the window. He looked at them. He meowed.

"Don't worry, Powder Puff," Dawn shouted. "We'll save you."

"We'll get you a mess of potato chips," Jason called.

"And some applesauce," said Dawn.

She rang the bell again.

They banged on the door.

Still no one came.

They sat down on the steps.

They could hear Powder Puff meowing.

"This is terrible," Dawn said.

"You're right," said Jason.

"Maybe we could walk around the back," Dawn said.

Jason waved his stick around.

"I'll take this just in case."

"Just in case . . . what?"

"Just in case we see a kidnapper."

They tiptoed down the driveway.

The yard was beautiful.

The grass was green.

"Look," Dawn said. "A zillion flowers."

Noni would love it.

A woman was kneeling on the grass. She was pulling out weeds.

She jumped when she saw them.

"We rang the bell," Dawn said.

"We knocked at the door too," said Jason.

The woman brushed her hair out of her eyes. She smiled at them. "Want to take a flower home?"

"Sure," Dawn said, "I want to take my cat home too."

The woman looked around. "I don't see a cat."

Dawn frowned. "It's a black cat," she said.

"It has a white ear," said Jason. "It has a white tip on its tail."

"I'm sorry," the woman said. "He's not here."

Dawn looked at Jason. "He doesn't like strangers," she said. "He likes to be in his own house."

The woman pulled at a weed.

It didn't come up.

"He'd probably bite a stranger," Jason said.

"He has very sharp teeth," said Dawn.

"My," said the woman. "He sounds tough."

"Tough as a tiger," Dawn said.

"Grrr," said Jason.

The woman pulled at the weed again. She pulled hard.

The weed came up.

The woman nearly fell over.

"My cat," said Dawn. "He's in your house."

"On your windowsill," said Jason.

The woman stood up quickly. "Goodness," she said. She brushed her hair out of her eyes again.

She started to run to the house. "Poor Blacky," she said.

Dawn and Jason ran after her.

"No," Dawn told her. "His name is Powder Puff."

The woman stopped at the back door. She turned the knob. "I'm coming, Blacky," she called.

She looked back at Dawn. "How did your cat get into my house?"

Dawn put one shoulder up. "He jumped into a car."

"Somebody else was driving, though," Jason said.

"I should hope so," said the woman. She stepped into her kitchen. "Here, Blacky. Mommy's here."

Dawn stood on tiptoes.

She looked into the kitchen.

She watched the big black cat come down the hall.

He jumped into the woman's arms.

"You're safe now," the woman told him.

She turned to Dawn and Jason. "Please get your cat off my windowsill. Get him out of here. I don't want him to hurt Blackie."

Dawn looked at the cat.

He was all black. Almost.

He had one white ear.

He didn't have a white tip on his tail, though.

Dawn pointed. "I thought that was my cat."

"I think I'd better sit down," said the woman.

"I think we'll look somewhere else," said Dawn.

"Some detective you are," said Jason.

···CHAPTER 6···

Jason was right, Dawn thought.

She was a terrible detective. Yucko.

She marched up to her bedroom.

It was hot up there.

Hot as an oven.

Powder Puff was stuck somewhere.

He was probably hot as an oven too.

Too bad cats didn't swim.

She'd take him to Emily Arrow's pool when she found him.

No. She shook her head. She'd keep him home, just the way Noni said.

She lay down on the floor.

She looked under her bed.

It was dusty under there.

She was supposed to clean it.

She always forgot.

She pulled out a box.

It was a polka-dot box.

A Polka Dot Private Eye box.

She opened it up.

It was time to think hard about being a detective.

It was time to find Powder Puff.

She took out her polka-dot hat.

It was a little big.

She put it on anyway.

It made her feel hot.

She felt as if a hippopotamus were sitting on her head.

A big fat one.

She looked inside the box.

A fake mustache.

Fake eyeglasses.

A magnifying glass.

Nothing that would help.

She pulled out the *Polka Dot Private Eye Book*.

She took it outside with her.

Jason was waiting on the lawn. He was waving his stick back and forth.

"Take that," he yelled.

"Aren't you worried about Powder Puff?" Dawn asked.

"Sure I am. I'm trying not to feel bad. That's why I'm playing. I'm fighting a guy with a sword."

He held the stick over his head. "The kind of guy who wears that tin stuff."

"You mean a knight," Dawn said. She

pushed her hat up. "We don't have time to play."

She sat there another minute. Then she opened her book.

"Some of this is just junk," said Jason.

He was looking over her shoulder.

"It is not," said Dawn. "It's great stuff."

"I don't see anything about a missing cat," said Jason.

"Here's what we need," said Dawn. "Scene of the crime."

"What?"

"That's where it happened. That's where the cat got lost. It's called the scene of the crime."

"What does it say?"

"Too bad you can't read better," said Dawn.

She looked back at him. "It says to write down everything you can remember."

She hopped up.

She went into the kitchen. A pencil was on the counter. She scooped it up.

She took a piece of Noni's THINGS TO DO TODAY paper too.

Noni wouldn't mind.

Outside she began to write.

1. Red car . . . mess.

2. Lady with mousetail . . . gray . . . carrying heavy box. Carrying pole.

3. Powder Puff jumped in car.

She chewed on the pencil. "That's all I can remember."

"What did the lady look like?" Jason asked. "Beside the mousetail?"

Dawn squinched her eyes shut.

She tried to remember.

"She was long and skinny," she said after a minute. "She was carrying a pole. . . . Hey." She picked up the pencil.

She began to write again.

4. Lady with mousetail . . . eating jelly cookie.

Dawn pushed her polka-dot hat up. "Put your stick away, Jason. I know what we have to do."

··· CHAPTER 7 ···

"Noni," Dawn yelled. "Where are you?"

Noni didn't answer.

Dawn ran into the house. She raced upstairs. "Noni?"

Noni popped her head out the bathroom door. "I'm trying to fix the sink. The water keeps dripping."

"Could I have some money?" Dawn asked.

Noni put her head on one side. "Why? How much?"

"For two jelly cookies. One for me. One for Jason."

"You want to walk to the bakery? On this hot day?"

Dawn nodded.

"Good," Noni said. "You can stop at the hardware store too."

"It's too hot," Dawn said.

Noni raised her eyebrows.

Dawn laughed.

"Get me a washer, please," Noni said. "It's this round thing." Noni held up a small plastic piece.

"I guess so," Dawn said.

Noni reached into her pocket. She pulled out two dollars. "I want the change back," she said. "Count it carefully."

Dawn raced down the stairs.

She waved the money at Jason.

"Come on," she said. "Let's go."

Jason followed her down the street. "Let's get ice cream instead."

Dawn slapped her head. "Jason. The mouse lady didn't buy ice cream. She bought a jelly cookie. We have to go to the bakery."

Jason stuck out his lip. "Maybe she likes jelly cookies. I like ice cream better."

Dawn sighed. She sat down on the sidewalk. "Listen, Jason. We are going to the bakery. We are going to ask the man if he knows the lady."

"The lady with the mousetail," Jason said. "Right?"

"Right."

"Good," said Jason. "After that we'll get ice cream." He grinned at Dawn.

Dawn started to laugh too. Then she looked up. "Yucko. That house."

Jason looked up too.

It was the house with the ladder.

Now someone was standing on the ladder. The painter had on a white hat. It had red stripes.

"Horrible green paint," said Dawn.

"Like spinach," Jason said.

Dawn tapped his shoulder. "Let's go."

They crossed the street. They turned the corner.

At Linden Avenue they stopped at the bakery. They looked in the window.

The sign said: CALVIN'S CAKES

A bunch of sugar cookies were piled in front.

A strawberry cake was in the back.

A wedding cake was in the middle.

"That wedding cake was here last week," said Dawn. She pressed her nose against the glass.

"It was here the week before that too," said Jason.

"Noni said it's just cardboard," Dawn said. "She said they stuck some icing on top."

"I'm never going to get married," Jason said.

Inside, Calvin was putting a jelly cookie into his mouth. "Best cookies in the world," he said.

"We wanted to ask you—" Dawn began.

"About the lady with the mousetail," Jason said.

Calvin put another cookie in his mouth. "No mice around here."

"No," said Dawn. "A lady. She has a long ponytail down her back. Did she come in here this morning?"

Calvin shook his head. "Sorry. I wasn't here. I slept late. Maybe my helper knows."

"Larry," he called to the back. "Who was here today?"

Larry poked his head out. "Bernie stopped in for a roll. So did Mrs. Simon. Mrs. Best bought a loaf of rye bread. Two or three boys came in. Then the painter."

Calvin nodded. "Larry has a good memory."

"Oh," said Larry. "The gas station man came in too."

Dawn sighed. "Have you seen any lost cats?"

"No." They shook their heads.

"Want to buy some cookies?" Calvin asked.

"No, thanks," Jason said before Dawn could answer. "We're going to get ice cream."

They went outside.

Dawn could hear Calvin talking to Larry. "My cookies are better than ice cream."

Dawn looked back. "I like your cookies too. I just can't eat them right now."

She felt like crying.

Suppose they never found Powder Puff?

···CHAPTER 8···

"You can eat a little ice cream," Jason said. "You don't even have to chew it."

"Well . . ." Dawn began. "I guess . . . Maybe."

They went into the ice-cream store.

Jason bought a two-stick orange ice-pop. Dawn bought a one-stick pop.

She'd buy another stick for Powder Puff if she found him.

They went outside again.

"Now what?" Jason asked. Orange ice dripped down his arm. He licked the bottom of the stick.

"Now I don't know," said Dawn. "I can't think of one thing."

"Maybe we should go in Emily Arrow's pool," he said. "We'll think better if we're nice and cool."

Dawn shook her head. "I have to keep looking."

They crossed Linden Avenue.

They started down the street.

"I'm all sticky," Jason said. "It feels terrible to be sticky and hot."

Dawn nodded. She ate the last of her ice. She was still thirsty. When she got home she'd ask Noni for a drink. A drink of ice-cold water.

Noni.

"Hey," Dawn said. "We forgot."

Jason looked at her.

"I'm supposed to get something for Noni."

She dug in her pocket. "It's a little round thing. It looks just like . . ."

She reached into her other pocket. "It's called a . . ."

She put her shoulders up in the air. "Can't find it."

"We'd better go to the hardware store anyway," Jason said. "We can ask Bernie about it."

They rushed back to Linden Avenue.

They turned in at the hardware store.

Bernie was behind the counter.

He was talking on the phone.

Dawn and Jason stood there waiting.

They waited a long time.

"We could be here forever," Dawn said.

"Let's look around," said Jason. "Maybe you'll find what you're looking for."

They went toward the back of the store.

The aisle was piled high. Pails. Circles of rope. Boxes of nails.

Dawn banged her knee on something. "Look," she said. "Snow shovels."

Jason lifted one. "I wish it were snowing right now," he said. "I'd lie down in it. I'd roll around. I'd . . ."

Dawn turned to the next aisle.

Cans of paint were piled almost to the ceiling.

She looked at the sign.

GREEN PAINT
BOX OF TWO CANS
HALF PRICE

No wonder that painter was painting the house green, Dawn thought.

Bernie came down the aisle. "Hi, Dawn."

"That's not such a great color," Dawn said. She pointed to the paint.

Bernie laughed. "I know. The painter bought some this morning, though."

"I need something for Noni," Dawn said. "What?"

She raised one shoulder. "I don't know. She needs it to fix the sink."

Bernie scratched his head. "A washer, I guess."

She followed him down the aisle.

She stepped over a paint roller.

She took the washer Bernie gave her.

She waited for Jason to come to the front of the store.

Then they started for home again.

Noni was in front of the house. She was waiting for them. "You forgot to take my washer."

"Don't worry," said Dawn. She held up the new washer.

"Good job," Noni said.

Dawn opened her mouth. "Hey, Noni. Jason. I just thought of something."

Noni smiled. "What?"

"I think . . . maybe . . . I know where Powder Puff is."

··· CHAPTER 9 ···

Dawn didn't wait to tell them about it.

She went into the kitchen.

She stood on a stool.

"What are you doing?" Noni asked.

Dawn grabbed a bag of potato chips. She waved them in the air. "Just in case," she said.

She jumped off the stool.

Noni sighed. She put the stool back. "You

have to put things away when you're finished."

Dawn reached up. She gave her a kiss. "Next time."

She raced out the door. "Come on, Jason."

Noni popped her head out. "Where are you going?"

"Not far," Dawn yelled back. "Not far at all."

They went down the street.

"Where are we going?" Jason asked.

Dawn turned the corner. "Right here."

"Right here?"

Dawn stopped to take a breath.

She pointed.

"I don't see anything," said Jason. "Not one thing."

"You see a house," said Dawn.

"A yuck green spinach house," said Jason.

Dawn went up the front path. She looked up.

The painter was up on the ladder.

The roller was on a pole. It was going up and down.

"Hey," Dawn yelled. "Do you have a car?"

"A red one. It looks like a mess." The painter pushed at the red striped hat. A long skinny tail of hair fell down the back.

It looked like a gray mousetail.

"Hey," said Jason. "A woman painter."

"Pauline," said the painter.

Dawn slapped her hat down on her head. "That's the name on the license plate."

The painter rolled some paint across the side of the house. "That's right," she said.

"But where's the car?" Dawn asked.

Pauline came down the ladder. She was carrying a can of green paint.

It was nearly empty.

She pointed with her thumb. "Car is out in back. In the shade. It's too hot in the driveway for my cat."

"Your cat?" Dawn gulped. "I lost mine."

"A gray cat?" Pauline asked.

Dawn shook her head. "No, black."

"White spot on his nose?"

Dawn shook her head again. "No, on his ear."

"Does he have a tip on his tail?" Pauline asked.

"Yes, a white one."

Pauline grinned. "This one has a green one. He got his tail in some paint." She leaned forward. "What's his name?"

"Powder Puff."

"Hmm," said Pauline. "I call my cat Jumper."

"That's a crazy name for a cat," Jason said.

"Crazy cat," said Pauline. "He jumped right into my car. He ate my lunch. He drank my soda."

Dawn took a step forward. "I think . . ."

Pauline was smiling at her. "I think so too."

"How did you guess?" Jason asked.

Dawn took a breath. "I knew Pauline was in the bakery. She was eating a cookie."

"Larry said the painter was in the bakery," Jason said.

"Right," said Dawn. "Then I saw the green paint at the hardware store."

Jason frowned. "I don't . . ."

"Pauline was carrying a box. A heavy one."

"Cans of paint," said Pauline.

"That's what I thought," said Dawn.

They went around to the back of the house.

Pauline's car was parked under a tree.

The windows were open wide.

Powder Puff was curled up on a pillow asleep.

"Good thing I'm a private eye," said Dawn. "This cat was probably lonesome for me."

"I'll miss this cat." Pauline smiled. "Wake up, Jumper," she said. "It's time to go home."